A novelization by Stephanie Calmenson
Based on the screenplay by Dennis Marks

SCHOLASTIC INC.
· New York Toronto London Auckland Sydney

A TURNER PICTURES WORLDWIDE RELEASE
TURNER ENTERTAINMENT CO. IN ASSOCIATION WITH WMG PRESENTS A FILM ROMAN PRODUCTION
"TOM AND JERRY – THE MOVIE" SCREENPLAY BY DENNIS MARKS SONGS BY HENRY MANCINI & LESLIE BRICUSSE
MUSICAL SCORE BY HENRY MANCINI MUSIC SUPERVISED BY SHARON BOYLE
EXECUTIVE PRODUCERS ROGER MAYER JACK PETRIK HANS BROCKMANN JUSTIN ACKERMAN
CREATIVE CONSULTANT JOSEPH BARBERA PRODUCED AND DIRECTED BY PHIL ROMAN

Original Motion Picture Soundtrack Album on M.C.A. Compact Discs and Cassettes   © 1993 TURNER ENTERTAINMENT CO. AND TELEFILM-ESSEN GMBH.

ISBN 0-590-47115-5

12 11 10 9 8 7 6 5 4 3 2 1   3 4 5 6 7 8/9

Printed in the U.S.A.   40

First Scholastic printing, July 1993

Contents

1.
Moving Day

On a city street filled with buildings made of glass and steel sits an old, white, wooden house. In the house lives a woman, her cat, and a mouse in the wall.

The house won't be there much longer. Soon it will be torn down. Another building made of glass and steel will take its place.

"Are you almost finished?" called the woman from the top of the stairs.

"Just about," answered a moving man as he lifted one end of a love seat.

"Don't forget the love seat!" said the woman.

"We got it!" groaned the moving man at the other end of the couch.

Then the woman called, "Tom! Thomas! It's time to go. Better hurry!"

Tom was the woman's cat. He shot up out of his basket. Oh, boy, he thought. This is it. Moving

1

day. He grabbed his food dish and his pillow. Then he zipped out the door.

On the way, he passed a hole in the wall. That was Jerry the mouse's house. Jerry peeked out. When the coast was clear, he grabbed his bag and his blanket and slipped outside after Tom.

Tom was just getting comfortable in the back of the woman's station wagon when he spotted Jerry. That mouse is not coming with me, thought Tom. No way. He reached for a pool cue that was lying in the back of the station wagon. Then he sat and waited.

As soon as Jerry hopped up into the car, Tom slid the pool cue between the mouse's tiny legs. He lifted Jerry up so the two of them were eye to eye.

Tom grinned from one end of his whiskers to the other. Then he curled two fingers together and — *FLICK* — he snapped Jerry off the pool cue.

Jerry didn't go very far. That's because he was hanging onto Tom's whiskers. Instead of flying out, Jerry flew backwards into the station wagon. It was Tom who went tumbling out, headfirst.

BOING! BOING! BOING! Tom bounced along the ground. When Jerry saw the look on Tom's face, he decided he'd better make a run for it. He jumped down from the station wagon, raced up across Tom's head, and then leaped off Tom's nose. He zipped inside the house to his hole in the wall and slammed the door behind him.

Jerry was leaning against the door of his house when the floor beneath him began to shake. *BAM! BAM! BAM!* He was lifted off his feet by the pounding at his door. *BAM! BAM! BAM!* Sharp, pointy nails came reaching in like cat claws.

I've got you now, you little mouse, thought Tom. He dropped his hammer and admired his work. He had nailed Jerry's house shut with boards.

Now Tom could travel the way he liked. *Uno.* Solo. Alone! He headed outside with a bounce in his step. I'd better hurry, he thought. I don't want to be left behind.

Tom looked out at the street where the station wagon had been. Gulp. The street was empty. The station wagon was gone. The moving van was gone. The woman was gone!

Tom looked down the street to the corner, just in time to see the station wagon's taillights disappear.

2.
Wham! Bam! Boom!

There wasn't a moment to lose. Tom ran down the street as fast as his legs could carry him. But when he turned the corner — *SCREECH!* — he stopped short. Standing right in front of him was a big, mean, ugly dog!

Tom put on his most winning smile. Then, before the dog knew what was happening, Tom had tied his ears in a bow across his big, mean, ugly eyes. Ready or not, here I go, thought Tom.

He raced home and slammed into the front door of his house. The door was locked. He could hear the dog getting closer and closer. Tom raced around to the back door. It was open. Thank goodness. Tom was safe!

He was also trapped. The dog was waiting for him outside, licking his chops.

No problem, thought Tom. I will stay right here, in my very own house. In fact, I will rest my head on this old pillow and take a nice snooze. He put the pillow on the floor and gently lay down his tired head.

BOING-OING-OING! A spring popped up from the pillow. It snapped Tom's head up and down, up and down, up and down. When his head stopped bouncing, Tom fell into an exhausted sleep.

The next morning, the sun came shining through the window. Tom was still sleeping peacefully in the living room. Jerry was sleeping peacefully in his hole in the wall. Even the mean, old dog was sleeping peacefully outside the door.

WHAM! BAM! BOOM! The dog yelped in fright and ran off. *WHAM! BAM! BOOM!* A wrecking ball came swinging through the living room window. The old, white house was about to come down.

Tom leaped up from his pillow and headed for the door. Chunks of the ceiling fell crashing down on him.

He was halfway down the block when he stopped in his tracks. Something was missing.

At that very moment, Jerry was pounding on the door of his little house, praying someone would save him.

Tom sighed, then raced back down the street to rescue Jerry. As they walked out of the house together, Jerry looked at Tom gratefully.

Neither of them saw the wrecking ball come swinging his way!

3.
Look Who's Talking

The wrecking ball scooped Tom and Jerry up into the air. Tom grabbed onto a tree branch with one hand. He held onto Jerry with the other. They watched as the wrecking ball continued on its way.

WHAMMMM! It hit the house one last time. All that was left of it were splinters and dust.

Tom and Jerry slowly climbed down from the tree. Seeing the old house go made them sad. They both wiped tears from their eyes. Then Tom started down the street, with Jerry following along behind.

Tom turned to Jerry, shook his head, and pointed in the other direction. Saving Jerry's life was one thing. Having Jerry follow him around town was another.

Jerry took a few steps the other way, then turned back and followed Tom when he wasn't looking.

By the time Tom reached the center of the city, his stomach was growling with hunger. He walked into the first restaurant he passed.

"No cats allowed!" shouted the owner. He picked Tom up by the scruff of his neck and dropped him on the sidewalk. Before Tom could get away, a street sweeper passed by, and Tom got an ice-cold shower.

Tom lay on the sidewalk in a dripping heap. The last creature he wanted to see staring him in the whiskers was that little mouse Jerry. And there Jerry was.

Tom stood up. He wrung his tail out on Jerry. Then he walked off in a huff. Soon he heard tiny footsteps behind him. He bent down and looked between his legs. Sure enough, it was Jerry.

Tom reached up to a window ledge and — *WHOMP!* — he brought a flowerpot down over Jerry. Jerry popped up out of the hole in the bottom of the pot. Tom pushed him down with his thumb. Jerry popped up. Tom pushed him down.

"Well, well, well. Look at the big, brave pussycat!" said a voice.

Tom twirled around to see where the voice was coming from. There was no one in sight.

"Big shot! Picking on a poor little teensy-weensy mousie!" said another voice.

8

Tom twirled the other way. He still did not see anyone.

"He'll feel guilty about this for the rest of his days," said the first voice.

Suddenly, from out of a beat-up old car came a beat-up old dog. "Instead of being pals, you're fighting like a cat and a mouse," said the dog.

"They *are* a cat and a mouse, Puggsy," said the second voice. Tom and Jerry still could not see where the second voice was coming from.

"That's true," said Puggsy. "But they've got to learn to be pals, or they won't make it out here. True, too?"

"All too true, too," said the second voice.

Just then, a dark speck jumped off Puggsy and landed on his nose. The speck was a flea. "Frankie Da Flea is the name. I'm French, of course," said the flea.

"That just means that before he met me, he lived on a poodle," said Puggsy. "We've been on the streets two years now. My owners left me behind when they moved. The name's Puggsy. What's yours?"

"I'm Tom," said Tom.

"I'm Jerry," said Jerry.

Tom and Jerry looked at each other, then cried out at the same time, "You talk!!!"

4.
Friends?

"Sure I talk! What do you think I am, a dummy?" said Tom.

"You said it, I didn't," answered Jerry, feeling pleased with himself for being so witty.

"You little pipsqueak!" said Tom, shaking his fists. "Why, I ought to . . ."

Suddenly Tom stopped. "Hey! How come you never spoke to me before?" he asked.

"There was nothing I wanted to say that I thought you'd understand," said Jerry. "So there."

Jerry turned his back on Tom and folded his arms across his chest.

"That does it! You get me so angry!" shouted Tom.

"Uh-uh-uh," said Puggsy, shaking his paw at Tom. "I told you before. You've got to be friends."

"Ab-sotive-a-lutely!" said Frankie from his seat

on Puggsy's cap. "We's been through thick and thin."

"And thin and thinner," added Puggsy.

"It's a dog-eat-dog world," said Frankie.

"That is *not* my favorite expression," said Puggsy.

"Oops. Sorry!" said Frankie. "Puggsy's right about being friends, fellas."

"Oh, boy. I don't know about all this friends stuff," said Tom. He and Jerry had always fought with each other.

"Well, what do you say, fellas?" said Puggsy.

Jerry put his hand out to shake with Tom.

Tom looked doubtful. "A cat and a mouse? Friends?" he said.

He thought for a minute, then folded his arms and turned his back. "No way! It's disgusting!" he said.

"That goes double for me!" said Jerry. He pulled back his hand and turned the other way.

5.
Trouble Everywhere

"You two don't want to be friends, that's your business," said Puggsy. "But we warned you. True, Frankie?"

"True, too," said Frankie.

"Hey, maybe you guys need a bite to eat. Follow me!" said Puggsy.

"Oh, boy!" said Jerry. "We eat!"

"Not you," said Tom. He picked Jerry up by the tail and dropped him back under the flowerpot. This time he put a cork in the hole so Jerry could not get out.

Tom followed Puggsy and Frankie down the alley. Puggsy grabbed a garbage can cover and held it up like a waiter's tray. He went from can to can, picking out treasures. "Hey, look. Chunky tuna. Pull up a tray, Tom," said Puggsy. "It's chow time!"

Tom was already deep into the next garbage

can. There was a half-empty sardine tin at the bottom.

"Hey, look over here, Frankie, boy," said Puggsy, lifting up a whole fish. "We hit the jackpot. . . . Urk!"

Suddenly, Puggsy, with Frankie on his shoulder, was yanked out of the alley. The two friends were thrown into the back of a large, black van. The drivers were wearing ski masks to cover their hideous faces.

"Heh-heh-heh! The Straycatchers strike again! Right, Lummox?" said the driver.

"Right, Abner. That's one more dog for the Doc," said Lummox.

Then the van shrieked off into the night.

Back in the alley, Tom found the fish on Puggsy's tray.

"Puggsy? Frankie? Where are you? Oh, well. More for me," said Tom when there was no answer.

CRASH! SMASH! Tom saw stars. His head had just been turned into a garbage can lid sandwich by the toughest alley cat he had ever seen. The alley cat and his tough friends surrounded Tom. They did not like him on their turf.

Tom stood tall and tried to act like a tough guy. At the same time, he inched his way backwards.

When he reached the fence, he made a run for it! The chase was on!

Five cats zipped through the fence after Tom. He took a flying leap over Jerry's flowerpot. The Alley Cats didn't see it. The first cat smashed into the pot, tipping it over. The other four cats piled up on top of the first.

"I'm outta here!" cried Jerry.

It didn't take long for the Alley Cats to get back on Tom's trail. Tom raced up one street and down another. He tumbled over a manhole cover with a rope attached to it. By the time he got up again, the Alley Cats were closing in on him.

When the cats reached the manhole, the cover popped up. The Alley Cats went down. *Gurgle. Gurgle. Ugh!*

Jerry let go of the rope he had tied to the cover. *CLANG!* The cover fell back in its place, trapping the Alley Cats.

Jerry put his hands on his hips and looked up at Tom, who had circled back when the Alley Cats disappeared. "You okay, pal?" asked Jerry.

"Yeah, but don't call me pal," said Tom, stomping away. He took a few steps, then stopped and looked back at Jerry. "Oh, all right, mouse. Come on!" he called.

Jerry made a fast U-turn. "Let's go!" he said. And he happily followed Tom down the street.

6.
Strangers in the Night

Tom and Jerry walked until they reached the river. It was dark out, and the moon's reflection was shining off the water.

They were about to cross an old bridge when they heard the soft patter of feet running along the cobblestones. A shadowy figure darted across the bridge. Tom and Jerry ducked out of sight and waited.

They heard the footsteps again on the other side of the bridge. In the streetlight, they caught a glimpse of a face. It was the face of a frightened little girl. She was running down the stairs to the river's edge.

"Pssst! Come on!" whispered Jerry.

Tom did not like the idea very much. He felt safe right where he was. But Jerry had saved him from the Alley Cats. So if Jerry wanted Tom to follow him now, it was the least he could do to pay him back.

Tom and Jerry hurried down the steps after the little girl. By the time they reached the bottom, she was out of sight.

WHOMP! Tom was hit in the face with a knapsack.

"Hold it! Hold it!" he cried.

"Who . . . who are you?" asked the little girl, coming out from beneath the steps.

"He's Tom, and I'm Jerry," said Jerry boldly.

"Oh. I thought you were somebody else. I was afraid you were following me," said the girl.

Tom and Jerry studied her in the lamplight. She was small and blonde and just about seven years old.

"What are you doing here?" she asked.

"We're lost and we're looking for something to eat," said Tom. "You see, we're kind of hungry."

Tom flashed his most winning smile.

"I've got some cookies in my knapsack. And an apple. You're welcome to have some," said the girl.

They sat down on the steps and ate and talked.

"So, why did you run away from home, Robyn?" asked Jerry.

"How did you know my name?" asked Robyn.

"It's on the locket you're wearing," said Jerry.

"Oh, yes. Well, I'm Robyn Starling. And I don't have a home. I'm an orphan," she said. "My father was on an expedition. There was an avalanche and . . . and . . ."

Tears fell as Robyn opened her locket. Inside was a picture of Robyn's father hugging her tenderly.

"He was the most wonderful father in the world. We had our own secret place for just the two of us. We called it Robyn's Nest. That's where I was going. To get away from my Aunt Figg. She's not *really* my aunt at all. She's just my guardian, but she's taken over the whole house. She moved me into the attic and gave my room to her dog, Ferdinand!" wept Robyn.

"That's awful!" said Tom, wiping a tear from his own cheek.

"She stole my locket and threw it out the window. But I climbed out and found it. Then I ran away. And I won't ever go back!" said Robyn.

"That's not too smart, kid," said Tom. "After all, you had a roof over your head, three meals a day, and a warm bed. You can't leave all that."

"He's right. You never know what you're missing till you don't have it," said Jerry.

"You don't know Aunt Figg. She *acts* sweet.

But she's mean. Really mean!" said Robyn.

"Ah, come on," said Jerry. "We'll take you home. You're better off there."

"That's right," said Tom. "Your aunt's probably crying her eyes out right this minute."

7.
Money Is a
Beautiful Word

"**B**oo-hoo-hoo! Boo-hoo-hoo!" sobbed Aunt Figg. "My poor little Robyn. You've got to find her, Officer. You've just got to!"

Aunt Figg's plump body and bright red hair shook as she wept. A highway patrolman stood with her in the library of the Starling mansion, trying to console her.

"There, there, lady," he said soothingly. "We'll find the little girl. I promise you."

"Thank you! I don't think I could live without her!" sobbed Aunt Figg.

"You *know* you *can't* live without her," said Mr. Lickboot, the family lawyer, as soon as the patrolman had left. "You need her money!"

"Shut up, you rotten weasel!" hissed Aunt Figg.

"It's true, Pristine. Without Robyn, Daddy Starling's trust fund money will go bye-bye and you'll be out in the cold-cold," said Lickboot.

"And I'll take you with me, you sniveling fool.

19

Think of something fast!" snarled Aunt Figg.

"Hee-hee-hee!" laughed Ferdinand, Aunt Figg's dog. He rolled out from under a table. Ferdinand was so fat and low to the ground, the only way he could get around was on a skateboard.

"It's all *your* fault, you fat freeloader! You let her get away!" said Aunt Figg.

"Yum-yum. Eating!" answered Ferdy.

"You're always eating!" said Aunt Figg. She threw a cupcake into the air. Ferdinand zoomed backwards and caught the cake in his mouth before crashing into the wall.

"Just pray the police find her, Pristine, or we'll be penniless," said Lickboot, stirring his tea. "And you'd better hope the rumor that Daddy Starling survived the avalanche isn't true. If he finds out how you've been treating Robyn . . ."

"Penniless? Did you say penniless?" said Aunt Figg, turning pale.

"Penniless! Bankrupt! Doomed!" said Lickboot.

"No! No!" said Aunt Figg. She began to pace. She did *not* want to be penniless. She had to find Robyn.

DING-DONG! A short time later, the doorbell rang. Aunt Figg opened the door to find Robyn, struggling to free herself from the highway patrolman.

"We found her down by the old bridge," said

20

the officer. "She's safe and sound."

"Thank goodness!" said Aunt Figg with a phony smile. "And who do we have here?" she asked sweetly, pointing behind Robyn.

"These are my new friends, Tom and Jerry. Can they stay here? Please? Please?" begged Robyn.

"It might be a good idea under the circumstances, ma'am," said the officer.

"Yes, of course, they can stay, darling," said Aunt Figg. "Thank you so much, Officer. You wouldn't be able to join us for a little celebration, would you?"

"Well," said the officer, "I sure would like . . ."

"Oh, I understand. You're much too busy. Good-night!" said Aunt Figg.

And she slammed the door in his face.

8.
Food Fight!

"Ferdy, show our new guests to the kitchen and give them something special to eat," said Aunt Figg with a gleam in her eye.

"Heh-heh. Special," drooled Ferdy.

He led Tom and Jerry to the kitchen. A feast was spread out on the table. There were turkeys, hams, pies, puddings, and cakes.

"Now that's what I call eats!" said Tom.

"Uh-uh!" said Ferdy. "*This* for you!"

He slid a bowl of smelly slop across the floor.

"*YECHH!*" said Tom and Jerry together.

Tom picked up the bowl of slop and sent it flying back to Ferdy. While Ferdy was busy wiping off the glop, Tom and Jerry jumped onto the table and began to eat. They were on their third course when Ferdy came at them, snorting like a bull.

"Food fight! Food fight!" called Tom.

Food went flying everywhere. In the end, Jerry was floating in a bowl of Jell-O, Tom was on the

22

floor licking peach pie and whipped cream off his whiskers, and Ferdy was laid out on the table like a turkey with the trimmings.

When Aunt Figg walked in, her cheeks turned three shades redder than her hair. "Oh, Robyn! Dearie! Get in here!" she barked.

Robyn came running down from the attic.

"As you can see, we have a little problem," said Aunt Figg. "Your housebroken pets have broken my house! I'm afraid we don't have room for them, after all. But don't worry. There's a sweet man down the street named Dr. Applecheek. He loves animals. Why, he just loves them to death!"

"Please don't send Tom and Jerry away! Please!!" begged Robyn.

"You can visit them every day," lied Aunt Figg. "And now, I must go talk with Mr. Lickboot, your daddy's . . . er . . . your dearly *departed* daddy's lawyer."

"Oh, Tom, will you mind very much going to Dr. Applecheek's house?" asked Robyn when Aunt Figg had gone.

"Hey, no. I'm a house kinda guy," said Tom.

"Jerry? Will you mind?" asked Robyn. "Jerry? Jerry? Where are you? Tom, Jerry's gone!"

"Maybe Ferdy ate him," said Tom.

"Don't even say that!" cried Robyn. "We've got to find Jerry before something happens to him!"

9.
He's Alive!

"**A** live??? What do you mean her father's alive?" shouted Aunt Figg as she paced back and forth in the library.

"The telegram just came," said Lickboot, handing it to Aunt Figg. "Daddy Starling is alive somewhere in the mountains of Tibet."

"Robyn must never find out," said Aunt Figg. "If she does, we won't see a penny!"

"Think positive. Maybe there'll be another avalanche. Maybe the Abominable Snowman will get him!" said Lickboot. "Maybe . . ."

THUMP!

"What was that?" said Lickboot, spinning around to where the noise came from.

Aunt Figg walked over to the bookcase and saw that her copy of *How to Be a Better Person* had fallen. She stood it back up. Luckily, she did not see Jerry. He was posed in a pirouette behind a ballerina bookend.

"Robyn must never find out," repeated Aunt Figg.

On the way out, she crumpled the telegram and tossed it into the fireplace. The paper bounced off a burning log and onto the bricks.

Jerry quickly slid down and rescued the telegram, whose edges had just started to burn. He raced down the hall to find Tom and Robyn. On the way, he passed under a dark shadow. The dark shadow stopped short.

Jerry looked up. Tom looked down.

"Hey, how'd you get there?" said Tom when he saw Jerry standing between his legs. "I've been looking all over for you."

"Read this!" cried Jerry, pushing the telegram in Tom's face. "Robyn's father is alive!"

"Daddy . . . blah, blah, blah . . . mountains of Tibet . . . blah, blah, blah," said Tom, speed-reading the telegram. "Hey! She's not an orphan no more! We've got to tell her!" Tom and Jerry raced up the stairs and hid in the shadows outside Robyn's room.

Up in the attic, Aunt Figg was putting Robyn to bed. "Good-night, little orphan. Sleep tight, little orphan," she said. "Don't let the scary things bite, little orphan!"

She closed the door with a bang and locked it.

Tom and Jerry stayed crouched in the corner

until Aunt Figg was out of sight. They waited a minute, then tiptoed to Robyn's door. Tom was reaching up to the doorknob when . . .

"How nice to see you!" cried Aunt Figg, jumping out of the dark. "Oh, look. You fetched my telegram from the fire. You are *so* helpful! I'll make sure Dr. Applecheek takes special care of you."

Aunt Figg grabbed Tom by the tail. "Get the mouse, Ferdy!" she called.

Ferdy caught Jerry in a jar.

The next thing they knew, Tom and Jerry were locked in a carrier and on their way to the home of Dr. J. Sweetface Applecheek.

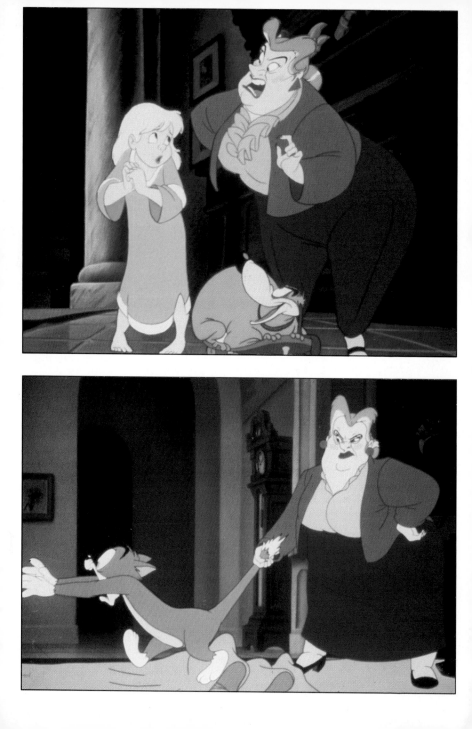

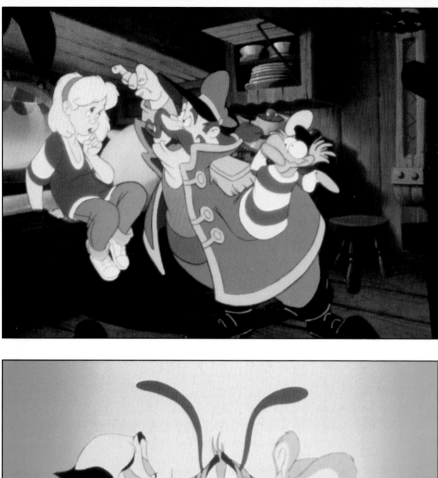

10.
Dr. Applecheek

"**Y**ou know what to do with them," said Aunt Figg, handing the carrier over to Dr. Applecheek.

"I'll take care of them," said the doctor as he led Aunt Figg out the door.

Tom and Jerry could see that Dr. Applecheek had rosy cheeks and a friendly smile. But there was more to Dr. Applecheek than met the eye.

"Let me show you my humble home," he said, grinning into the carrier. As he walked through the house, Dr. Applecheek's grin turned into an evil scowl. He opened the door to the basement. Then, passing down the carrier, he called, "Here they are, boys. Get rid of them tonight."

The next thing Tom and Jerry knew, Abner and Lummox, the hideous Straycatchers, were locking them inside a cramped and smelly cage. All around them, animals were whimpering and moaning.

"Hey, look who's here!" said a familiar voice.

"I see! I see!" said another familiar voice.

"Puggsy! Frankie!" called Tom. "What are you guys doing here?"

"The Straycatchers grabbed us from the alley," said Puggsy. "How about you?"

Tom and Jerry told Puggsy and Frankie about their battle with the Alley Cats and how they met Robyn under the bridge. They told them her whole sad story.

"Her Aunt Figg says she's an orphan, but she isn't. Her daddy's alive, only she don't know it yet," said Tom. "We gotta bust outta here and tell her!"

"We gotta bust outta here anyway. This Dr. Applecheek kidnaps pets. Then he sells them back to their owners for lots of money. Or he breeds them and sells the puppies. Or, if they're run-of-the-mill types like us, he finishes them off for good!" said Puggsy.

"Leave it to me, Frankie Da Flea. I'll get us outta here," said Frankie.

As soon as Lummox and Abner were asleep, Frankie slipped out of Puggsy's cage and found the control panel that locked all the cages. "Ugh! Oof!" groaned Frankie in the dark.

"How ya doin'?" asked Puggsy.

"I almost got it," said Frankie.

28

"Ugh! Oof!" Frankie groaned again and again, pouncing up and down on the buttons. Finally, one cage door swung open. Then another. And another.

At first, the animals were too stunned to move. Then Puggsy called, "Okay, everybody out!"

All the dogs, cats, and birds leaped from their cages. They ran over Abner and Lummox. Then they headed upstairs and trampled Dr. Applecheek.

"Yeowwww!" he cried. Dr. Applecheek spun round and round and round. He ended up with his head stuck in a dog cage and his feet waving in the air behind him.

"We did it!" cried Puggsy. "Go give the little girl her good news!"

"Thanks! We're on our way!" said Tom and Jerry. And they disappeared into the night.

11.
Reward!

A s soon as she heard the news that her dad was alive in Tibet, Robyn started packing her bags.

"Do you know how far away Tibet is?" asked Tom.

"It's far," said Jerry. "It's way past Cleveland!"

"I don't care. I'm going," said Robyn.

She knotted her sheets together to make a rope. Then she tied one end to the bedpost and tossed the other end out the window.

Robyn climbed out first. Tom, with Jerry sitting on his head, followed right behind. They swung down the rope, past Aunt Figg's window.

Aunt Figg, in her nightgown and pink curlers, heard a rustling at her window. At first she thought it was just the wind in the trees. Then she sat up in bed and muttered, "Something's wrong."

By the time she made it up to the attic, Robyn,

Tom, and Jerry were well on their way to the river.

"What's that over there?" asked Robyn when they got to the water. She was pointing to a dark object floating under the bridge.

"It looks like an old crate," said Tom.

Jerry ran ahead to inspect it. "Wrong," he said. "It's our raft!"

"Shh! Listen!" said Robyn.

They heard car tires rolling through the gravel. Then they heard doors opening and closing. Next they heard a voice. It was Aunt Figg!

"This is where they found her last time," she was saying to Lickboot. "She'll come here again. I know it!"

Ferdy began sniffing the air. "Robyn-Fratz. Whacka-whacka! Yah!"

"Oh, hush, Ferdy," growled Aunt Figg.

Under the bridge, Robyn's eyes opened wide with fear. "Get on the raft and keep quiet!"

Tom, Jerry, and Robyn squeezed onto the raft and pushed off. They were carried off by the current, far from shore.

When Aunt Figg could not find them, she left.

Hours passed. Robyn, Tom, and Jerry were fast asleep, drifting down the river when . . .

Putt-putt. Putt-putt. A boat in the distance came heading their way.

PUTT-PUTT. PUTT-PUTT. It was a huge fishing boat. The captain did not see the raft on the dark water.

SMASH! CRASH! The fishing boat hit the raft and split it in two.

"HELP!!!" cried Robyn, Tom, and Jerry.

While the raft was coming apart on the river, Aunt Figg was coming apart back home. "What do you mean there'll be no more money!" she screamed into the telephone.

"If we can't prove we're taking good care of Robyn, we can't touch another penny of her father's money," said Lickboot at the other end.

"Then get her back. Do anything! Lie, cheat, steal!" cried Aunt Figg.

There was a minute of silence at the other end. Then Lickboot said, "I've got it. We'll offer a reward. One million dollars. Someone will turn her in for sure."

"We don't have a million dollars!" said Aunt Figg.

"No problem," said Lickboot. "I'll just lie, cheat, and steal."

"Get busy!" said Aunt Figg.

Lickboot made the necessary calls. By morning, Robyn Starling's picture would be on every milk carton in the country with the words: ROBYN

STARLING MISSING! ONE MILLION DOL-
LARS REWARD!!!

When all that was arranged, Lickboot made one more call. It was a call Aunt Figg knew nothing about.

"Hello, operator. I want to place a long distance call — to Tibet!"

12.
Captain Kiddie

After the crash, Robyn drifted down the river, unconscious. When she woke up, she was inside a trailer filled with circus posters. A scruffy parrot sat on a countertop, staring at her.

"Aaawk!" cried the parrot.

"Aaaaah!" cried Robyn.

"Aaawk!" cried the parrot.

"Aaaaah!' cried Robyn.

"Great wobbling wattles!" said an odd-looking man with a sea captain's hat on his head.

He pulled the parrot puppet from his hand.

"You scared me with that thing!" said Robyn.

"Sorry, my dear," said the man. "How are you feeling? You gave us quite a fright. You've been lying here for three days."

"Where am I?" asked Robyn.

"You're with me! Captain Kiddie, of Captain Kiddie's Carnival. I'm King of the County Fair, Pirate of Pleasure. And this is my first mate,

Squawk," said the captain. "Say, are you hungry?"

"Am I ever!" said Robyn, feeling more relaxed.

"I'll rustle up some cookies and milk for you, matey. It'll just be a minute," said the captain.

Captain Kiddie was pouring the milk when he saw it. The face on the carton. It was Robyn's face. And the words: ONE MILLION DOLLARS REWARD!!!

"Will you excuse us for a moment, my dear?" said Captain Kiddie, handing Robyn a glass of milk and some cookies with a trembling hand. "I need to speak outside with my first mate."

"Of course," said Robyn, biting into a cookie.

Captain Kiddie raced down to the water. "We're rich! We're rich! We're rich!" he shouted, waving the carton in the air.

"Rich-aawk! Rich-aawk!" screeched Squawk the puppet.

Captain Kiddie threw the carton back over his head as he kicked up his heels and danced his way back to the trailer.

Tom and Jerry lay flat on the ground, watching the odd-looking man with his bird puppet. After the crash, they had drifted along the river for days. They had made it to shore early that morning.

As soon as they landed, Jerry saw something

glimmering in the weeds. It was Robyn's locket. That meant she had to be somewhere close by.

Tom reached for the milk carton. "Oh, boy! Something to eat that isn't fish!" he said.

He opened the carton and started to drink. *Gulp. Gulp. Gulp. Gulp.*

"Hey!" said Jerry.

"Oh, sorry," said Tom. "Here, have some."

"No, look! It's Robyn!" said Jerry.

"Where, where?" asked Tom, spinning around.

"Right here! On the milk carton!" said Jerry.

Tom looked at the carton. "You're right! It's her! And it says there's a million-dollar . . . wow! You don't suppose . . ."

"I sure do suppose," said Jerry.

"I didn't like the look of that guy. Or his bird, either," said Tom.

"Robyn's here. And we've got to find her. Fast!" said Jerry.

13.
Step on It!

"**I**t's all your fault!" cried Dr. Applecheek, storming through the door of the Starling mansion.

"*My* fault?" hissed Aunt Figg. "If you had done away with that cat and mouse like I paid you to do, the little brat wouldn't have run away again."

"Those two animals have cost me a bundle," said Dr. Applecheek. "Not to mention the damage . . ."

Brrrring! Brrrring!

"Wait here," said Aunt Figg, glaring at Dr. Applecheek. "I'll be right back."

Aunt Figg disappeared inside the library and slid the door closed behind her. Dr. Applecheek waited outside until his curiosity got the better of him. He slid the library door open just wide enough to hear Aunt Figg speaking into the phone.

"Yes? Yes? Yes! I did offer a one-million-dollar

reward for the return of my precious little Robyn. Where is she?"

Aunt Figg grabbed a pencil and wrote in big letters as she repeated the name: CAPTAIN KIDDIE'S CARNIVAL.

"I've got it. I'll be right there!" said Aunt Figg, hanging up the phone. She tried not to hit her head on the ceiling as she jumped for joy.

"Yes, yes! Yesss! We did it!" she cried.

She pulled herself together before going back out into the hallway.

"Now, Doctor, you were saying something about damages. Doctor? Doctor?" called Aunt Figg.

"Step on it, Abner!" said Dr. Applecheek as he jumped into the Straycatchers' van. "We've got to get to Captain Kiddie's Carnival. One million dollars is ours if we do."

As they tore out of the driveway, they passed Lickboot's red sports car heading in the other direction.

"You're just in time!" cried Aunt Figg when Lickboot pulled up to the door. "Robyn's at a place called Captain Kiddie's Carnival. We've got to get there on the double! Step on it!"

Ferdy scooted out of the mansion on his skateboard and hopped up onto the backseat.

"We'll be there before you can say one million

dollars!" said Lickboot, stepping on the accelerator.

Aunt Figg and Ferdy flew back in their seats as the car screeched out onto the road.

The Straycatchers' van was holding its lead up ahead.

"So, boss. How much of the million dollars are we going to get?" asked Lummox.

"Get? You? You get nothing!" roared Dr. Applecheek. "If you two had finished off that cat and mouse like I ordered, we wouldn't be in this fix!"

SCREECH! The van lurched to a stop. The door to the van opened, and Dr. Applecheek tumbled out onto the curb. Then the van sped off again down the road.

"Come back! Come back! We'll share everything fifty-fifty! Make that sixty-forty! We'll make a deal!" cried Dr. Applecheek.

Just then, Lickboot's red sports car zipped by. Dr. Applecheek went wild! He had to get back on the road. He just had to!

At the corner, he spotted a vendor selling ice cream to children from his motorcycle-driven ice-cream cart. Dr. Applecheek's eyes shone as he headed toward it.

"The party's over, kiddies," he said.

14.
Get Her!

"**H**ow about a ride on Captain Kiddie's Ferris wheel?" said the captain.

"Oh, yes! I love Ferris wheels," said Robyn.

Captain Kiddie helped her into a seat and handed her a red balloon. "Here's a little company," he said, locking the seat bar in place. "Have a safe trip, my dear."

"That's right. We wouldn't want anything to happen to Robyn Starling," mumbled Squawk.

"I heard that!" cried Robyn in a flash. "How did you know my name? I never told you!"

"Sorry, kid," said Captain Kiddie as he pulled the switch. "We're keeping you here till your aunt comes to get you."

The Ferris wheel's motor began to grind. The Ferris wheel chugged around until Robyn was swinging from the top.

"Please! Please let me down. Don't send me back to Aunt Figg. She hates me!" called Robyn.

But the captain wasn't listening. He was already asleep at the controls.

Robyn sat alone crying in her rickety seat in the air. When she went to wipe away her tears, she lost hold of her balloon, and it floated away.

A few hours later, the balloon came floating back.

"How can that be?" wondered Robyn. Something was hanging from the end of the string. She reached for it. "My locket!" she cried, grabbing hold of it.

She looked down and saw Tom and Jerry waving up to her. They were signaling her to be quiet.

Robyn mouthed the words, "Aunt Figg is coming!"

Tom and Jerry nodded to let her know they understood. Then they got to work.

Tom climbed on top of the ticket booth, while Jerry slipped in beside Captain Kiddie at the controls. Then Tom lowered a fishing hook to Jerry. He hooked it under the cuff of Captain Kiddie's pants, and Tom reeled him in!

"Great wobbling wattles! All hands on deck!" shouted the captain as his chair toppled back.

"Aawk!" shouted Squawk.

"Get them!" cried the captain, untangling himself from the fishing hook. Tom made a run for it, with the captain and Squawk on his trail. Meantime, Jerry pulled the switch and brought Robyn down.

The captain and Squawk were stopped in their tracks when a red sports car pulled up in front of them.

"Where's the girl?" demanded Aunt Figg.

"The money first!" said the captain.

"After we see Robyn. Where is she?" asked Lickboot.

SCREECH! It was the Straycatchers' van!

"You're too late! I got here first," Aunt Figg called to Lummox and Abner. She spun back around to Captain Kiddie. "Now where is she?"

"Up there," he said, pointing to the Ferris wheel.

"Let's get her!" cried Lummox.

Robyn was just reaching the ground when Abner and Lummox came charging. She lifted the seat bar and jumped out, just as they leaped into her car.

Jerry quickly flicked the controls, slamming the seat bar back down. Lummox and Abner were trapped. They went flying into the air.

"Uh-oh!" cried Jerry. "Look who's coming!"

Aunt Figg, Ferdy, Lickboot, Captain Kiddie, and Squawk were all heading their way.

"There's the little brat!" cried Aunt Figg. "Get her!"

15.
Ahoy, Mates

"Quick, they're getting away!" cried Lickboot. Tom, Jerry, and Robyn leaped onto Captain Kiddie's paddleboat.

Tom pushed every button and flicked every switch on the control panel. He was trying to find the one that would start the boat.

"Push the red button. It's *always* the red button!" said Jerry.

"Hey, I knew that," said Tom.

He pushed the red button. The boat lurched forward and chugged away, throwing off a mighty spray that drenched Aunt Figg.

"I'll get the car!" said Lickboot. "We'll head them off up the river!"

"Do something, Captain! We're in a race for a million! Awwk!" screeched Squawk.

"Watch this!" said Captain Kiddie. He pulled a rubber dinghy with a powerful motor out from under the pier.

Ding-a-ling-a-ling! Just then, Dr. Applecheek pulled up to the carnival in his motorcycle-driven ice-cream cart.

"Hey, Doc, we're up here!" called Abner from the top of the Ferris wheel.

"Good. Stay there!" said Dr. Applecheek. He locked the Ferris wheel into place and headed down the road after Aunt Figg.

"They're all following us!" cried Robyn. "Step on it!"

"It won't help," said Tom. "Look."

The words "Low Steam" were flashing in red on the control board.

"Don't worry. We can fix it," said Jerry.

Tom and Jerry ran down to the lower level of the boat and started shoveling wood into the firebox.

Meantime, alongside the river, Lickboot missed a turn in the road.

"Watch out!" cried Aunt Figg as they plowed through a fence and into a clothesline.

"How can I watch out? I can't see anything!" cried Lickboot, with a pair of undershorts draped over his head.

The car landed with a splash in a pigsty.

"Yucka-yucka, ugh!" cried Ferdy as he went flying out of the car and into the mud.

Ding-a-ling-a-ling! Dr. Applecheek waved to

Aunt Figg as he drove through the path Lickboot had made for him.

"Applecheek is getting ahead of us. Hurry, Lickboot!" shouted Aunt Figg.

Lickboot stepped on the gas, but the wheels just churned in the mud of the pigsty, burying Ferdy in a mountain of goop.

By the time they freed themselves, Captain Kiddie, with his powerful motor running at full blast, was closing in on the paddleboat. "Ahoy, mates! Prepare to be boarded!" he called.

"Awwwk!" cried Squawk.

"Oh, no!" cried Robyn. "He's going to get us for sure!"

16.
Fire!

Wham! Captain Kiddie was so busy watching the paddleboat, he didn't see the bridge ahead of him. His boat slammed into the side of it.

Ding-a-ling-a-ling! Applecheek's motorbike was racing up onto the bridge. He was almost close enough to jump onto the paddleboat when he hit a bump and flew over the side.

He landed on top of Captain Kiddie's dinghy, and they all went down into the water and disappeared.

"Good-bye forever!" called Tom as the paddleboat sailed away.

"Tom! Jerry! I know where we are!" said Robyn. "We're heading toward Robyn's Nest, my special place. That's where Daddy would look for me if he thought I was in trouble. Maybe he's there now!"

When the paddleboat reached the pier, Robyn jumped off ahead of Tom and Jerry. She ran straight to the cabin and flung the door open. A lamp on a table threw a shadow across the room. "Daddy! Daddy, is that you?" asked Robyn.

"Daddy is dead," said a voice. It was the voice of Aunt Figg.

"No-ooo-ooo!" screamed Robyn.

"If you know what's good for you, you'll never run away again," said Lickboot.

"You're not taking me back. You'll *never* take me back!" cried Robyn.

"Oh, yes, we will," said Lickboot, grabbing Robyn's arm.

"Tom! Jerry! Help me!" cried Robyn.

"We're coming!" called Jerry.

They were banging on the door, trying to get in, but it was locked.

Robyn gave Lickboot a kick in the shin. "Take that!" she said.

"Ow, ow, ow," said Lickboot, grabbing his shin and hopping around the room. "Why, you little . . ."

Robyn kicked Lickboot in the other shin. He staggered backwards, knocking into a table.

"Look out!" yelled Aunt Figg.

The lantern on the table fell over and exploded

on the floor. Kerosene streamed across the cabin. It made its way to the curtains. The curtains burst into flame.

"Help!! Help!! Fire!!" cried Robyn. She headed for the stairs leading up to the loft.

"No, Robyn! You've got to get out. The house is burning down!" called Lickboot.

"I won't go with you. You'll *never* take me back!" cried Robyn.

"Lickboot, let's get out of here!" shouted Aunt Figg.

"But what about the girl?" asked Lickboot.

"Forget her! We've got to save ourselves!" answered Aunt Figg. She ran for the door, with Ferdy close at her heels. But the lock was jammed.

Robyn, Aunt Figg, Ferdy, and Lickboot were trapped in the burning cabin.

"Tom, Jerry, where are you?" coughed Robyn as the smoke drifted up to her.

.

17.
Daddy!

Lickboot came out of the kitchen, waving a key. "Give it to me!" shouted Aunt Figg.

Aunt Figg grabbed the key from Lickboot. She grabbed it so hard, the key ring broke open, sending all the keys flying across the floor.

Aunt Figg and Lickboot scrambled to find the one they needed. But there was so much smoke, they could hardly see past their hands.

"I've got it!" cried Aunt Figg. She jumped up and tripped backwards over Lickboot. They both fell into the door, knocking it off its hinges.

"We're out!" yelled Lickboot.

"Yeow! Ow! Out!" barked Ferdy, who was right at Lickboot's heels.

Lickboot stood up. He stepped on Ferdy's skateboard. Ferdy flipped up into the air and landed on Aunt Figg. Aunt Figg stumbled backwards into Lickboot. And they all went *bumpity-bump-bump-bump* down the cabin stairs.

"Oh . . . oh . . . no!" yelled Lickboot as he landed in the crow's nest of Captain Kiddie's paddleboat. Aunt Figg landed in his lap.

Ferdy landed on the throttle, and the engine started up. The paddles began to turn, and the boat started humming off down the river.

BAM! BAM! BAM! Robyn, who was still trapped up in the loft, heard someone banging above her. She looked up toward the skylight. It was Tom and Jerry. "Thank goodness!" she cried.

They pulled open the skylight and threw a rope down to Robyn. She grabbed the rope and swung up and out over the sea of flames. Off in the distance, they could hear the whirring of a helicopter.

"Someone must have seen the flames. Help is on the way!" said Jerry.

When the helicopter reached the cabin, it began circling overhead.

Robyn heard a voice calling, "Hang on, Robyn! I'm coming down to get you!"

"It's Daddy!" she shouted. "Daddy! Daddy!"

The helicopter came lower and lower. Robyn, Tom, and Jerry huddled together against the wind.

"Robyn, take my hand. Hurry!" shouted Daddy over the noise of the helicopter.

Robyn reached out and was swooped up in the air. "Oh, Daddy, I knew you'd come!" said Robyn.

"You're safe now. I'm here," said Daddy.

The helicopter turned and started back up into the air.

"No! Wait! We can't leave Tom and Jerry!" cried Robyn, looking back toward the cabin.

Suddenly, a burst of flame shot up into the air. The roof of the cabin gave way, and Tom and Jerry disappeared down into the smoke and flames.

18.
Little Buddy, Little Pal

"Tom! Jerry!" cried Robyn.

She watched the cabin get swallowed up by flames, then crumble to the ground in a heap.

"Oh, Daddy, they're gone! My best friends are gone!" cried Robyn.

"Please don't cry, Robyn. We'll find them," said Daddy.

He turned the helicopter around and circled back toward the ruins.

Meantime, down in the river, a bubble broke the surface. Then another. And another.

Glub, glub, glub.

Tom's head came rushing up from under the water. He thrashed around, gasping for air. When he could finally breathe again, he began to search for Jerry.

Pieces of the cabin were floating along the river. Tom knew Jerry could be under any one of them.

He threw them up out of the water, sending them flying every which way.

"Jerry! Jerry, where are you? Oh, don't leave me, little buddy. You've got to be here. What would I do without you? You were the best pal a guy could ever have. Oh, little buddy, little pal, please be alive. I promise you . . . ah, let's see, I promise you . . ."

"All the cheese I can eat," said a voice floating by on a soap dish.

"All the cheese you can eat," said Tom. "And . . . and . . ."

"And no more traps," said the voice.

"And no more traps!" said Tom.

"And no tricks?" said the voice.

"And no tricks," repeated Tom.

"That's a promise?" asked the voice.

"That's a . . . hey . . . what's going on here?" said Tom. He finally realized that a voice in the darkness was feeding him his lines.

Tom turned round and round in the dark water. Then, in the light of the fire, he saw Jerry floating in front of him. Jerry waved.

"Hey, buddy!" Jerry said.

"Why, you little . . . don't you call me buddy!" shouted Tom.

"Pal?" asked Jerry.

"I oughta . . . I oughta . . ." said Tom, shaking his fists.

Then his fists changed into outstretched hands. He picked Jerry up and gave him a great, big kiss.

"Boy, I'm glad to see you, little buddy, little pal!" said Tom.

Just then, the wind from the helicopter started whipping around them.

"Look, Daddy, there they are!" called Robyn. "Tom! Jerry! You're safe!"

The helicopter landed, and Robyn ran out onto the pier. Then the three friends gathered together in a wet, happy hug.

19.
Bye-bye

Aunt Figg, Ferdy, and Lickboot were watching everything from their perch in the paddleboat.

"That's so sickening," said Aunt Figg. She was still gasping for air from the fire. Suddenly, a look of horror came across her face.

"What is Starling doing here? Who told him his precious little girl was in trouble?" snarled Aunt Figg.

Lickboot tried to back away, but there was nowhere to go. He spit a fish out of his mouth and spluttered, "He . . . he would have found out anyway!"

Aunt Figg's eyes opened wide. "You!!! You told him?" she shouted.

"A lawyer's got to look out for himself every now and then," said Lickboot, bracing himself.

"You double-crossing, bottom-feeding, mud-sucking, garbage-eating, gutless, low-down, no-good lawyer!" shouted Aunt Figg, beating him over the head with her fists.

"Grrrr!!!" growled Ferdy, tugging at Lickboot's pant leg.

"Ouch! Oooh! Oh! Please!" yelled Lickboot.

While Aunt Figg was pounding Lickboot over the head, Ferdy quietly steered the paddleboat out onto the river.

"Lickboot-fratz, bye-bye," snarled Ferdy.

They sailed past Captain Kiddie's Carnival, where Lummox and Abner were still hanging in the air on the Ferris wheel.

"Help us! Somebody, please help us!" shouted Lummox.

"Get us down! I'm afraid of heights!" called Abner.

But the paddleboat just sailed past them down the river.

20.
Boy, What a Team

The next day at the Starling mansion, Tom, Jerry, and Robyn were saying good-bye to Puggsy and Frankie.

"Are you sure you won't stay?" asked Robyn.

"Nah, you know us. The open road, a million new tomorrows," said Puggsy.

"And a pal to share them with," said Frankie from his seat on Puggsy's nose. With that, the two friends set off down the road.

Tom, Jerry, and Robyn watched them disappear, then went back inside the mansion.

"Welcome to your new home!" said Robyn. "Make yourselves comfortable," she said. "I'm going to visit with Daddy. I'll see you guys later."

She showed Tom to his cozy, new bed and Jerry to his new mousehole, which had its own awning and red carpet.

Jerry went to the door of his new house and stood there for a moment admiring it. It was just like the door to the mansion. "Home, sweet home," he said.

"Allow me," said Tom. He opened the little wooden door for Jerry. Then he bowed and, with a wave of his arm, pointed him inside.

"Why, thanks, pal," said Jerry. He walked into his house and was about to sit down when he saw a mousetrap come sliding in.

Tom sat outside, grinning from whisker to whisker. He was waiting for the delicious sound of the trap snapping on Jerry's tail.

He could feel his own tail flipping in happy anticipation. *SNAP!!* "Yeowee!" cried Tom.

Jerry had slid the mousetrap back outside. He jumped for joy when Tom's tail flopped down onto it.

"Why you little . . ." cried Tom. He started running after Jerry. "I'm gonna get you!"

"Maybe you will," said Jerry. "And then again, maybe you won't."

As they raced around the house, it seemed just like old times.